SAVED BY THE SMELL

JARRETT LERNER

ALADDIN
New York   Amsterdam/Antwerp   London
Toronto   Sydney/Melbourne   New Delhi

This book is a work of fiction. Any references to historical events, real people, or real places are used fictitiously. Other names, characters, places, and events are products of the author's imagination, and any resemblance to actual events or places or persons, living or dead, is entirely coincidental.

ALADDIN
An imprint of Simon & Schuster Children's Publishing Division
1230 Avenue of the Americas, New York, New York 10020
First Aladdin hardcover edition March 2025
© 2025 by Jarrett Lerner
Jacket design by Karin Paprocki
Also available in an Aladdin paperback edition.
All rights reserved, including the right of reproduction in whole or in part in any form.
ALADDIN and related logo are registered trademarks of Simon & Schuster, LLC.
For information about special discounts for bulk purchases, please contact Simon & Schuster Special Sales at 1-866-506-1949 or business@simonandschuster.com.
The Simon & Schuster Speakers Bureau can bring authors to your live event. For more information or to book an event, contact the Simon & Schuster Speakers Bureau at 1-866-248-3049 or visit our website at www.simonspeakers.com.
Interior design by Irene Vandervoort
The illustrations for this book were rendered digitally.
The text of this book was set in Haboro Soft and Kabouter.
Manufactured in the United States of America 0125 BVG
10 9 8 7 6 5 4 3 2 1
Library of Congress Cataloging-in-Publication Data
Names: Lerner, Jarrett, author, illustrator.
Title: Saved by the smell / by Jarrett Lerner.
Description: First Aladdin edition. | New York : Aladdin, 2025. | Series: My mad scientist mom ; 1 | Audience: Ages 5 to 8. | Summary: Ari's life takes a chaotic turn when his mad scientist mom devises a portal to tackle their overwhelming laundry crisis, leading to much bigger problems when they accidentally travel 70 million years back in time.
Identifiers: LCCN 2024033503 (print) | LCCN 2024033504 (ebook) | ISBN 9781665942980 (pbk) | ISBN 9781665942973 (hc) | ISBN 9781665942997 (ebook)
Subjects: CYAC: Mothers and sons—Fiction. | Family life—Fiction. | Time travel—Fiction. | Scientists—Fiction.
Classification: LCC PZ7.1.L4685 Sav 2025 (print) | LCC PZ7.1.L4685 (ebook) | DDC [Fic]—dc23
LC record available at https://lccn.loc.gov/2024033503
LC ebook record available at https://lccn.loc.gov/2024033504

FOR MOM

Chapter One

I WAS IN THE KITCHEN, FEEDING FRED. HE'S MY pet turtle. And if you know anything about turtles, you probably know that they take.

Their.

Time.

So you can imagine how long it takes the little guy to eat a piece of lettuce.

Not that I really cared. I didn't have

anything better to do with my day. My mom and I had moved to this new town a couple of months ago, and I hadn't really made a friend yet. And, I mean, even if I *had* made a friend, I definitely wouldn't have invited them over to our house on a Saturday afternoon. That would've been an awesome way to *lose* that friend of mine nice and fast.

I'd spent most of the day playing video games, which is fun, and also a great way of distracting yourself from the fact that you've been in a new town for two whole months and still haven't made a single friend. But then Mom had called up from the basement and told me that I should take a break from the TV and, just to be safe, that I should also stay a few feet away from any other electronics. She was working on something downstairs, and according to her there was "a slight to moderate risk" that "a large to enormous" electric current could shoot out of an outlet and into *me*.

Anyway, Fred was almost done with his lettuce when—DING-DONG—the doorbell rang.

I tipped my ear toward the basement door, wondering if Mom was expecting someone.

But all I heard was something that sounded like hammering, followed by Mom shouting, "Stubborn thing!"

I turned back to Fred.

"You okay for a minute?" I asked him.

He slow-motion wrestled the last morsel of lettuce into his mouth.

"I'll take that as a yes," I said.

I pushed my chair back and got to my feet.

"Coming!" I called out as I headed for the door.

Chapter Two

I OPENED THE DOOR, AND THERE, STANDING on our front steps, was a bald guy.

Actually, he wasn't completely bald. He had these little tufts of hair that poked up from behind each of his ears. And he also had a mustache—a bushy one that hung down a bit over his lips.

I should probably say, this bald guy

wasn't a total stranger. It was Mr. Jakes. He lived in the house right next to Mom and me. It was only him in there. Though I think he had a cat. Or maybe two? I don't know. The guy could've had *a hundred cats* in that house with him.

All I knew was that Mr. Jakes was always coming around *our* house. He'd ring the doorbell, or knock on the side door, or just show up on the lawn if Mom and I happened to be out there. He'd say something about the weather. Or tell us about the little step stool he's got, then ask us if we needed help changing a lightbulb, reaching something on a high shelf, or dusting the tops of our kitchen cabinets.

Today Mr. Jakes was carrying a big plastic container. The plastic was green, but see-through enough that I could make out a bunch of stacks of cookies inside. Chocolate chip, it seemed.

Mr. Jakes looked at me, then leaned to the side so he could peer *past* me.

"Um," I said, to grab his attention back. "Can I help you?"

Mr. Jakes gave an awkward little laugh. Then he held up the container of cookies and said, "I was baking, and I—I suppose I got a bit carried away. I, ah—I made too many. Does Susan—I mean, your mother—does your mother—does she, er, enjoy cookies? Does she enjoy oatmeal raisin cookies?"

My stomach turned.

Because *oatmeal raisin*?

Yuck.

I wanted to tell Mr. Jakes that *no one*

enjoyed oatmeal raisin cookies—especially not after they had mistaken those chewy little globs of dried fruit for *chocolate chips.*

But I didn't want to be rude. The guy was odd, for sure—but he was nice enough.

So I said, "Maybe?"

I held out a hand, and Mr. Jakes passed me the cookies.

"Thanks," I told him, giving the door a shove.

As the door swung shut, Mr. Jakes leaned to the side again to see into our house. And it sort of seemed like he was about to say something else. But whatever it was, the door closed before he could spit it out.

I turned around, but only made it a single step back toward the kitchen.

That was when the lights began to flicker.

And then I heard it:

The unmistakable sound of an explosion.

Chapter Three

IT WAS A SMALL EXPLOSION.

But still *an explosion*.

Which is usually not something you want to hear coming from *inside your house*.

I hurried the rest of the way back to the kitchen, where I scooped up Fred, set him atop Mr. Jakes's cookie container, and rushed toward the basement stairs. I barreled down the things—but then, a few steps from the bottom, I froze.

Why?

Because when it came to my mom, you could never be sure what you were about to get yourself into.

Was I going to take those last steps, turn the corner into the basement—and find myself facing an enormous lava-hot laser beam?

Or was I going to turn the corner—and walk right into a thick blue cloud of ice-cold sleeping gas?

Both of those things had happened to me. And during *the same weekend*.

Because my mom . . .

She's a . . .

Well . . .

She's a MAD SCIENTIST!

But wait.

Before you go and get the wrong idea, let me explain.

Mom's not *angry* all the time. She's probably the *least* angry person I know. She's one of those people who always wake up happy. Every single day. It doesn't matter if she looks out the window and see's the sun shining or if instead she sees dark, gloomy clouds and sheets of bleak rain. Or even if she wakes up and sees that our backyard is mysteriously *engulfed in flames*. (Yes, that happened too. It was over that *same* weekend I mentioned before, believe it or not, and had to do with

Mom's laser beam malfunctioning.) Mom can look at any situation and right away, pretty much automatically find the bright side.

It's like, *Oh, the backyard is mysteriously engulfed in flames? How convenient! I was planning on getting rid of the grass and putting in a patio anyway. Now, where in the world did I put the hose?*

Anyway, it's not because of Mom's *mood* that she's known as a mad scientist.

It's because of her work—her experiments and inventions. They're all a little bit . . . *out there.*

Or, okay, maybe *a lot bit* out there.

She does things that other scientists consider silly, preposterous, or just plain KOOKY.

And I know all this because "silly," "preposterous," and "just plain KOOKY" are all things other scientists have called both

Mom and her work in their science magazines.

I don't think that's entirely fair, though. Because if you look at Mom's experiments and inventions from a different perspective— if you try to look at them like she looks at the world—you could just as easily call them "innovative," "groundbreaking," or "cutting-edge" (or any of the other dozen synonyms I found on our computer's thesaurus app). Instead of seeing Mom as a mad scientist, you could see her as a bighearted genius. Someone who wants to make people's lives better by solving the sorts of problems that all those *other* scientists usually overlook.

And that's how *I* see her.

Most of the time, at least.

Because it can be hard to think like Mom when the power's out, a minor explosion just rocked your house, and you're about to turn the corner into a basement where you've got no clue what kind of dangerous situation is waiting for you.

Chapter Four

I TIGHTENED MY GRIP ON MR. JAKES'S COOKIE container, checked on Fred, and took those last steps and turned the corner into the basement.

Then I shrieked.

It was only Mom.

But she was standing *right there*, just a couple of inches away from me, and I guess I

was already on edge. I mean, even when our power was working fine, the basement wasn't the most welcoming space. There were a couple of small storm windows for some sunlight to squeeze in through. But other than that, the place was gloomy, and absolutely jam-packed with Mom's equipment, in-progress experiments, and half-built contraptions.

All that combined with the fact that

I often found laser beams and clouds of sleeping gas when I went down there—and, well, if you'd been in my sneakers, I bet *you* would've shrieked too.

Not Fred, though.

The little guy and that last stubborn lick of lettuce (he was *still* chewing the thing) were in a world all their own.

Mom glanced down at Fred, then tipped her head to better peer into Mr. Jakes's cookie container.

"Mr. Jakes?" she asked.

"Mm-hmm," I answered.

"Chocolate chip?"

I shook my head. "Oatmeal raisin."

One of Mom's eyebrows shot up. The other one sank down, nearly squinching her eye shut.

"Interesting," she said.

Then she cleared her throat, and the curious look on her face was replaced by a much more serious one.

"Ari . . . ," Mom said.

I gulped.

"Yes?" I asked.

Mom said, "You and I have got ourselves a *problem*."

I'd been afraid of that.

Chapter Five

IN THE HANDFUL OF SECONDS BETWEEN WHEN Mom told me she and I had a problem and her telling me what that problem was, I hoped for two things:

    1. that the problem was *not* the kind that would put our lives at risk (like the time she tried to turn our regular old car into the "self-driving" kind, or when she outfitted our vacuum cleaner with a "turbo" button), and

2. that the problem *was* the kind that we could get someone else to deal with.

When it came to asking other people for help, though, Mom didn't have the greatest track record. She tended to see problems, whatever they were, as *challenges*—and ones that *she* wanted to overcome. But now and again something would break and she'd be too busy with one of her projects to take it on herself. And *that's* what I was hoping for. That we could call up an electrician or a plumber or whatever, make an appointment, and then go back to our regularly scheduled lives.

But then Mom said, "Our problem, Ari, is a *laundry problem*."

And maybe you're thinking that as soon as I heard that, my heart rate slowed. Maybe you're assuming that I felt I could suddenly breathe easy.

Because, a laundry problem?

Big deal.

How could laundry possibly be dangerous?

Well, if you're thinking any of that stuff, then you clearly don't know my mom....

Anyway, after Mom told me what our problem was, I peered around the basement. And as dim as it was down there, I saw right away what she was talking about. I quickly counted more than a dozen piles of dirty clothes, some of which had apparently been there long enough for Mom to start using them as makeshift tables. I noticed an open notebook balanced atop a heap of T-shirts. Beside it, a beaker full of purple liquid was nestled into a mound of socks.

"I'm currently wearing my last clean lab coat," Mom told me. "And you, my sweet," she added, "started smelling funky four days ago."

My eyes leapt back over to her.

"I—I did?"

"In fact, it was nearer to four and one quarter days ago," said another voice. It had a fancy accent, and sounded muffled, like it was coming from inside someone's pocket. That's because it was coming from inside someone's pocket.

Mom reached into her lab coat and pulled out TED. The ice-cube-sized supercomputer hovered an inch or so above Mom's flattened hand, looking down at me in that super snobby way of his.

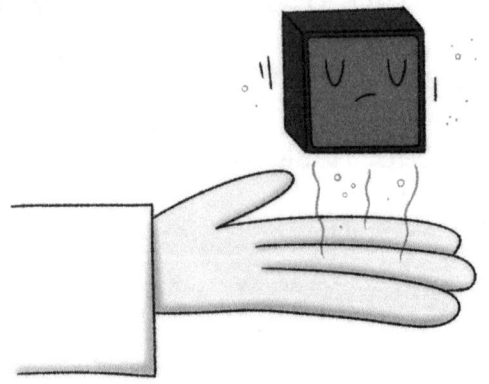

Mom had designed, built, and programmed TED herself. His name was an acronym, which meant each letter stood for a different word. But I could never remember what the words were. All I knew was that Mom *should've* named the thing TMAAUSITW, which stands for "The Most Annoying and Useless Supercomputer in the World."

"Go on," TED said, glancing down at my T-shirt. "Smell for yourself."

I lowered my head and gave myself a sniff. And, unfortunately, Mom and TED were right. I smelled like I'd just gotten done playing an epic game of dodgeball . . . on a farm . . . with a bunch of particularly unhygienic pigs.

When I looked back up, Mom had thankfully stuffed TED back into her pocket. Now she had her hands on her hips and her chin tilted up. She was standing there in our dreary, cluttered basement, right beneath a lightbulb that had just blown, like a superhero would stand before they flew off to save the world.

Mom said, "But have no fear, my dear. Our laundry problem is as good as solved." She lifted a single finger and poked it high into the air. "For I have devised a most elegant solution."

My stomach twisted up in anxious anticipation.

Then Mom stepped aside and pointed to the far end of the basement. And there, beyond the little mountain range of dirty clothing, I saw something that had definitely *not* been in our basement the day before.

It was a metal frame, roughly the size

and shape of a refrigerator. And inside the frame, curling inward from each of the four corners, was a patch of slowly swirling, faintly glowing, purply-pink air.

Chapter Six

THE FIRST THING I DID AFTER SPOTTING THE mysterious new object at the far end of our basement was put down Mr. Jakes's cookie container. Then I grabbed Fred and got him set up on a bit of empty floor nearby. And *then* I looked back over at the thing—or, I guess, mostly at the purply air contained within it.

For a minute I couldn't speak. That patch of swirling air was super distracting. Mesmerizing, even.

But then, finally, I managed to find my voice and ask Mom:

"WHAT IS THAT?!"

Mom grinned.

"*That,*" she told me, "is a time portal. And from now on it'll be doing our laundry for us."

Living with my mom, you hear a lot of weird things. Some of the sentences that come out of her mouth—I'm willing to bet that no one else on planet Earth has ever been in a position to say them. But "from now on the TIME PORTAL will be doing our laundry for us"? Well, that might've been the weirdest thing I'd heard her say yet.

"But . . . ," I said, trying to wrap my head around the situation I now found myself in the middle of. "But *why*? We've got a perfectly good washing machine."

"Correction," Mom said. "We *used to have* a perfectly good washing machine."

I turned around and looked over at the other side of the basement. And there, past a few more piles of dirty clothing, I saw our washing machine. Or what was left of the poor thing. It looked like it had tumbled down a couple hundred flights of stairs.

"How did *that* happen?" I asked.

"That is neither here nor there," Mom said, grabbing my shoulder and spinning me back around. "Because we now have no need for a washing machine. We have"—she swung one arm out toward her new creation, sort of like she was a salesperson trying to get me to make a big purchase—"a time portal."

Then she cleared her throat and explained.

"You see, Ari, by adjusting the speed, direction, and force of the energy contained within the time portal, you and I can *travel back in time*. Specifically, we can travel back to six weeks ago, which is the last time we washed, dried, and folded our laundry."

Mom's voice softened.

"Don't you remember it?" she asked me. "All those T-shirts and lab coats lined up neatly on the couch, smelling like a field of wildflowers?"

"I remember it," said a muffled, snobby-sounding voice. "It was precisely six weeks, three days, seventeen hours, twenty-nine minutes, and seven seconds ago. Now six weeks, three days, seventeen hours, twenty-nine minutes, and eleven seconds ago. Now—"

"That's enough, TED," Mom said, patting the supercomputer in her pocket.

(Remember when I said TED was annoying? Yeah. . . .)

"In any case," Mom said, "that's all there is to it. You and I will pop back in time, gather up all the clean clothes we can carry, then come right back here. And just like that—problem solved! I'll have plenty of clean lab coats, and *you* won't smell like a hockey player's unwashed sock." Mom leaned a little closer to me, gave a sniff, and grimaced. "That for some reason has been stuffed full of very old cheese." She sniffed once more. "And mustard."

I took a step back before she could add anything else to her description.

Then I took a deep breath and summoned all the brainpower I could.

I was going to need it.

Chapter Seven

I HAD FOUND MYSELF IN THIS SITUATION BEFORE.

Hold on—let me clarify.

I had never found myself in the situation in which my mom had built a time portal and suggested we use it to travel back in time in order to gather up a bunch of clean clothes so we never again had to do our laundry.

But I *had* found myself in plenty of situations

in which my mom wanted to do something utterly outrageous and wildly dangerous and I had to try to convince her *not* to.

And that's exactly what I tried to do.

"Mom," I said, "couldn't we just go and buy a new washing machine?"

She frowned at me like *I* was the one who was proposing something preposterous.

"We could," she said. "But that would be a waste of money. The time portal will do our laundry for us. *And*—I haven't even gotten to this part yet—it won't use a single drop of water. It's better for the environment, too!" She grinned, obviously ecstatic.

"But—but—but—" I said, scanning the basement, hoping I'd see something that'd give me another idea. Because my mom was a genius, there was no doubt about that, but I still wasn't exactly *eager* to mess around with a homemade time machine.

Finally my eyes landed on Fred, and on the cookie container near him.

"Mr. Jakes!" I said. "He must have a washing machine! We could use his!"

Amazingly, Mom didn't immediately argue against this. She seemed to actually be seriously considering spending the day at our neighbor's house doing load after load of laundry. And if I'd only given her another couple of seconds to think it over, she might've even given in.

But I pushed it.

I just *had* to open my mouth and say, "I mean, it *would* be way easier."

And as soon as that last word left my lips, I knew I'd messed everything up.

Mom's face took on a look of steely determination.

"Progress," she told me, not for the first time, "does not happen *easily*, Ari." She swung around to face the time portal. "And you and I, sweetie pie, are about to forever change the way people do their laundry."

Before I could say another word, Mom reached into the pocket of her lab coat—the one that TED wasn't in—and pulled out a remote control. She thumbed at the buttons and—**FWIIIIIRP!**—the air swirling inside the time portal slowed to a stop before it—

SHHHWWOWOWOWOWOWOW

—started spinning in the opposite direction.

Mom dropped the remote back into her pocket.

"Ready?" she asked me, pulling her goggles down over her eyes.

My heart sped up to a gallop.

"NOW?" I said. "We're doing this RIGHT NOW?!"

Mom glanced at me over her shoulder. "That T-shirt isn't getting any better-smelling," she said, crossing the basement and stepping right up to the portal. "Now remember, honey," she called back to me, "grab as many clean clothes as you can. And no dillydallying. We don't want the portal to close up on us."

"CLOSE UP ON US?! MOM! I—"

But that's all I said.

Because that's when Mom leapt into the portal and, with a soft sort of slurping sound, disappeared.

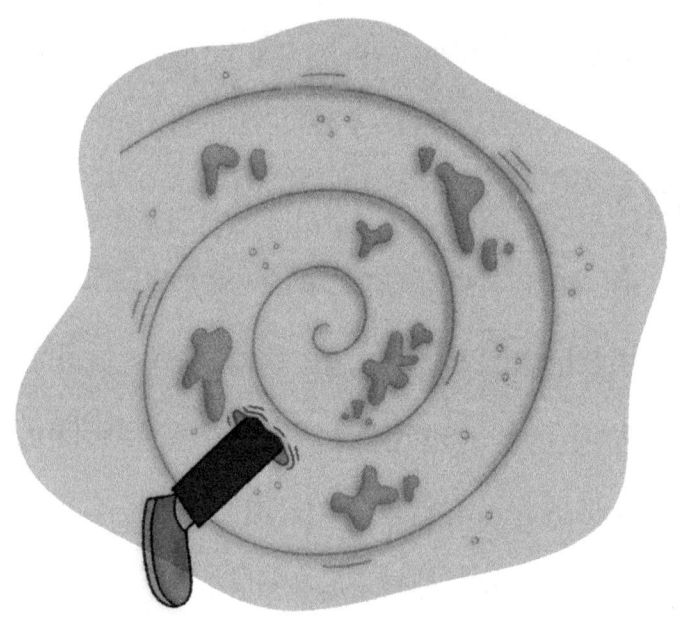

And what choice did that leave me?

I crossed the basement, scared out of my mind.

Then I leapt into the portal too.

Chapter Eight

YOU'RE PROBABLY WONDERING WHAT IT FEELS like to travel through a time portal.

The answer: not so great.

It was sort of like being on a merry-go-round—but a merry-go-round spinning at about six hundred miles per hour. Also, instead of there being gentle, tinkly music playing, it's like you've got your ear pressed up to a roaring airplane engine.

Oh!

How could I forget?

It also messes with your body. It feels sort of like your limbs have all been turned into dough, and like a team of professional weight lifters are trying their hardest to yank your arms and legs right out of their sockets.

The only *not-so-terrible* thing about traveling through the time portal was that it didn't last very long.

After maybe seven seconds, all of it—the spinning, the roaring, the yanking—abruptly stopped.

Then I was falling.

I swung my body around and spotted the ground.

Right before I slammed into it.

A big puff of dirt flew up all around me, blowing into my eyes, up my nose, and coating the inside of my mouth.

I waited for the air to clear a bit. Then I pushed myself up onto my knees and climbed to my feet.

Swatting away the last of the dust, I looked around.

Here's what I saw:

Dirt.

Rocks.

Trees.

Some mountains in the distance.

A few long, thin clouds stretching out overhead along with a brightly burning sun.

Here's what I *didn't* see:

Our basement.

Our clothes.

Anything at all that was even *remotely familiar*.

I also couldn't see MY MOM.

Which was why, for the second time that day, I opened my mouth wide and shrieked.

Chapter Nine

SO THERE I WAS, SHRIEKING.

Until . . .

"ARI!"

I swung around.

Mom was standing right behind me. She was as dirty and dusty as I was, and the look on her face? Let's just say she didn't seem quite as confident as she had *before* we'd both hopped into the time portal. She looked a little confused. But mostly—and much more scarily—she looked *concerned*.

"Ari," she said. "It would appear I made a miscalculation somewhere or other."

"Uh," I said, "*yeah*. You think?"

Mom peered around some more. She narrowed her eyes at one of the nearby trees.

Then she bent down and picked up a rock.

After a minute she dropped the rock. It hit the ground and rolled a few feet away.

Mom brushed her hand off on the side of her lab coat. Then she said, "It seems we may have traveled a tad further than six weeks into the past. I suspect we have gone back more like"—she paused, and winced at me before finishing her sentence—"sixty million years."

Chapter Ten

WHEN I HEARD WHAT MOM SAID, IT WAS LIKE my brain went through a time portal of its own. It was spinning and stretching, trying to make sense of the words that had come out of her mouth.

Trying—and *failing*.

Because sixty million years?

It was one of those gargantuan hunks of

time that the human mind can't really make sense of.

I felt panic coming on.

But before it could really take hold, I swung around and started searching the empty landscape surrounding us.

"Where is it?" I said. "Behind that rock?"

"Where's *what*?" Mom asked.

"The—the thingy," I said, growing more and more agitated because I couldn't find it. "The time portal."

"Er . . . ," was all Mom said.

But something about the way she said it stopped me cold. Slowly, I turned to face her.

She looked extremely nervous about what she had to tell me next.

"It doesn't really work like that," she said. "The time portal can't travel *with* us."

The worry began to fade from Mom's face as she got carried away with her scientific explanation.

All of a sudden Mom and I were no longer having a conversation. Instead it was like I was sitting in school, listening to a teacher give a lecture.

This sort of thing happened a lot.

"In order to make a return trip, so to speak," she went on, "we need to establish a *loop*. Establishing a loop requires—"

"*Mom,*" I said, stopping her there.

Her eyes popped open. Then she blinked hard. I think, for a second, she'd completely forgotten that we'd *accidentally traveled sixty million years into the past.*

Nice and slowly I asked, "Are you saying that we're *stuck*?"

Mom took a deep breath. Then she said, "Temporarily . . . yes."

That was when I lost it.

Chapter Eleven

THE PANIC THAT HAD BEEN BUILDING UP INSIDE me was blown aside by a surge of an even more intense emotion:

Anger.

"I *knew* something like this would happen!" I shouted. I was pacing back and forth in front of Mom, kicking up my own personal dust storm, swinging my foot at any rock that was unlucky enough to be in my way. "Something like this *always* happens. We can never just do the normal thing. We always have to make it *hard*. We always have to make it *dangerous*. It's like a day isn't actually a day unless something somehow goes spectacularly wrong. And bonus points if we almost *die*."

"Ari—" Mom tried to say.

But I was way too worked up to listen.

I kept pacing, and kept shouting, too.

"*Why*, Mom? Why can't we *just once* do the *easy* thing? The *normal* thing? Huh?"

I stopped and turned to face her. Then I waited a second, letting the air clear so Mom could see me glaring. "Why can't *you* just be a *normal mom*?"

I said it—and right away I wished I could take it back. Especially after I saw how, hearing it, Mom's whole face fell.

"Mom . . . ," I said, my voice now barely a whisper. And then I started to say something else, something about how I hadn't truly meant it. But the truth was that I kind of *did* mean it. I *did* wish Mom was more normal. Not *all* the time. But some of the time, yeah. And as much as I wanted to hurry up and get that hurt look off Mom's face, in that moment, lying to her felt like it might only make things worse.

So I changed the subject instead.

I said, "Are you *sure*?"

Mom frowned at me, confused.

"Maybe you're wrong," I explained. "Maybe we *didn't* actually go back sixty million years." Then something else occurred to me. "Get TED! Get him out! Ask TED!"

Mom hesitated. But then she reached into her pocket and pulled out the supercomputer.

"TED," I said, practically breathless. For

the first time in my life, I was actually glad to see the annoying little know-it-all. "Mom thinks we accidentally traveled sixty million years back in time. Did we?"

The supercomputer blinked its tiny electronic eyes. Then it ticked them back and forth, taking in our surroundings, using the wires and chips or whatever was inside him to perform countless calculations per second.

At last TED said, "Professor Fingerman is incorrect."

I let out a breath I hadn't even realized I'd been holding.

But then TED said, "I estimate that we have, in fact, traveled closer to *seventy* million years back in time."

My heart skipped a couple of beats.

Then it started racing like it was being chased by a pack of wolves.

"I believe," TED continued, "that we find ourselves squarely within the Cretaceous period."

Usually when TED used a big word that I didn't know the meaning of, I just got irritated. (And then, later on, I'd look up the word in the dictionary so he couldn't do it to me again.) But this word "Cretaceous" sounded familiar. I knew I'd heard it before, somewhere or other.

"Cretaceous?" I said, hoping that saying it out loud might help me remember. Because it was like the word had hunkered down in the middle of my brain. Like, until I figured out where I'd heard it and what it meant, I wasn't going to be able to think about anything else—even the fact that we were apparently an *extra ten million years* away from home. "Creta—"

It hit me all of a sudden.

"Wait a second," I said. "Isn't the Cretaceous period when there were dino—"

That was as far as I got.

Because that was when a deafening sound tore through the air.

"RRRRRAAAAAWWWWRRRR!"

Chapter Twelve

THE ROAR WAS SO LOUD, IT LITERALLY SHOOK the ground. Pebbles and rocks bounced up into the air, and even some of the bigger boulders jiggled. The trees got it too. Leaves and even entire branches toppled out of trees, then quivered around in the dirt.

Mom planted a hand on my shoulder and

held on tight, steadying me. If she hadn't, I might've fallen over myself.

Then, as abruptly as it had started, the roar stopped.

Somehow, though, the silence *after* the roar was even scarier than the roar itself.

I was way too terrified to turn and look.

But Mom tightened her grip on my shoulder and slowly spun me around, forcing me to see.

And there it was, off in the distance, about the length of a soccer field away.

A *dinosaur.*

Hold on.

I know you might be eager to keep reading and find out what happened next.

But I want to make sure you properly appreciate what I just said. I want you to try to put yourself in my sneakers, to imagine yourself standing at one end of a soccer-field-sized space and seeing an enormous dinosaur at the other.

Are you doing it?

Do you kind of, sort of feel like you're really there?

Can you see the creature's rippled, scaly skin?

What about the patches of crusty mud along its sides?

And the spit—do you see the rope

of gooey saliva dangling from the thing's gigantic jaws?

Okay.

Now imagine the dinosaur cranking its head to the side.

Imagine one of its little yellowy eyes rolling around before aiming itself in *your* direction and coming to a sudden stop.

And, finally, imagine the creature—more quickly than you could've ever believed was

possible—twisting itself about and beginning to run right at you.

BOOM! BOOM! BOOM!

The ground was shaking all over again.

"Professor Fingerman?"

It was TED, who was still hovering above the hand that Mom didn't have on my shoulder. His voice was wobbly, unlike I'd ever heard it before.

"I would very much like to be put back into your pocket now," the supercomputer said.

Mom tucked TED into her lab coat. Then she said, "Ari, *RUN!*"

Chapter Thirteen

MOM AND I RAN.

We ran like our lives depended on it.

Because, you know, they *did*.

The problem was that we didn't really have anywhere to run *to*. There was a handful of boulders and here and there a tree. And yeah, a bunch of them were big enough to hide behind. But hiding *behind* something didn't seem good enough. Not when there was a massive, angry-sounding dinosaur coming after us.

"MOM!" I cried out. "WHAT DO WE DO?"

She didn't answer.

So I looked over, and saw that, as she was running, she was fiddling with a remote control—the same one she'd used back in our basement to work the time portal.

"MOM!" I tried again.

This time she called back, "I JUST NEED TO SET UP A LOOP! ONCE I DO THAT, WE CAN GET BACK! OR AT LEAST GET OUT OF HERE!"

I still wasn't entirely clear on what a "loop" was and how it worked. But that didn't keep me from wanting her to hurry up and do it.

"SO GO!" I urged her, glancing back over my shoulder to see that the dinosaur was gaining on us. "DO IT! SET UP A LOOP! SET UP A LOOP!"

"I'M TRYING!" Mom told me. "IT'S RATHER DIFFICULT," she added, her thumbs twitching atop the remote control, pounding button after button. "ESPECIALLY WHILE RUNNING LIKE THI—"

Mom must've tripped over a rock. Because the next thing I knew she was lurching forward.

She managed to keep herself from slamming into the ground. But in the process of getting herself balanced, she bobbled the remote. And somehow, even though we were hurtling forward at full speed, the next few seconds seemed to happen in slow motion.

The remote tumbled out of Mom's hands...

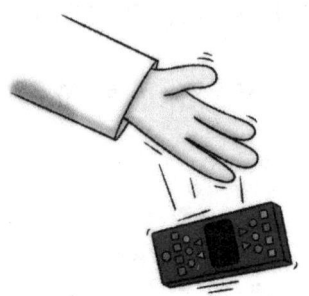

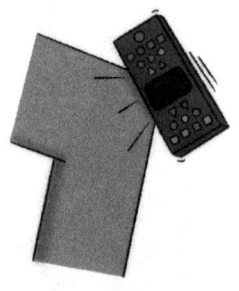

And struck her knee...

Which sent it flipping up into the air...

And bonking off her forehead . . .

Which caused it to hurtle down toward the ground . . .

Where it landed . . .

And where Mom, her eyes still shut following that bonk on the forehead, accidentally stepped on it with a sickening CRUNCH!

Mom froze.

I skidded to a stop a few feet in front of her.

We locked eyes.

She looked more panicked than I'd ever seen her before.

With the dinosaur's stomps getting

louder and louder, shaking the ground more and more, Mom lifted her foot.

And I didn't need to be a genius with a bunch of scientific expertise to know that the remote control was totally busted.

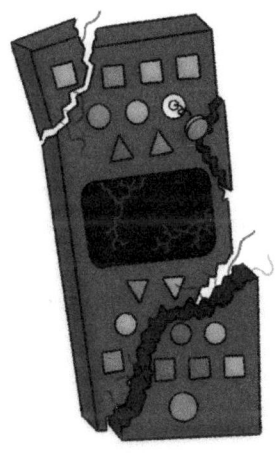

The thing definitely wasn't going to be helping us set up a loop anytime soon.

Meanwhile, behind us:

"RRRRRAAAAAWWWWRRRR!"

The dinosaur wasn't slowing down. In a handful of seconds, it'd be close enough to snatch us up in its nightmarishly enormous jaws.

Mom dropped to her knees and scooped up the pieces of the remote. She shoved them into her lab coat, then popped back up onto her feet.

"There!" she said, pointing to one of the nearest boulders. And when I didn't start running right away, she grabbed on to my stinky T-shirt and tugged me along after her.

Chapter Fourteen

FORTUNATELY, MOM AND I MADE IT TO THE boulder before the dinosaur made it to *us*. We crouched low and huddled close, making ourselves as small as possible. The boulder was barely big enough to keep us out of sight.

"I don't know a great deal about dinosaurian intelligence," Mom whispered. "But

perhaps this one lacks object permanence. If we're lucky, the creature will forget we're here and go look for a snack elsewhere."

I widened my eyes to let her know I'd heard her. I was too afraid to move any more than that.

BOOM!

The dinosaur was still stomping closer— but it sounded like it was slowing down.

BA-BOOM-BOOM-BOOM!

And then the stomping—and BOOMing—stopped.

I hardly breathed, anxious that even the almost nonexistent sound of air moving into and out of my lungs might attract the dinosaur's attention.

But beside me Mom was carefully rearranging her arms and legs so that she could reach into her pocket.

She pulled out TED.

And the supercomputer looked how I felt: *terrified*. I hadn't even known he could make that kind of expression.

"TED," Mom said quietly, "I'm going to hold you up. Tell us what you see."

The supercomputer's mouth fell open, like he was going to protest. But before he could get a word out, Mom lifted her hand so it was even with the top of the boulder we were tucked behind.

I watched TED bob an inch or so higher into the air.

"What do you see?" Mom asked in a whisper. "Is the dinosaur still there?"

"I see . . . ," began TED.

And what he said next?

Well, it was *not* what I'd been expecting.

He said, "Fred?"

Chapter Fifteen

WHEN TED SAID "FRED," I WAS SO SURPRISED TO hear the name of my pet turtle that I nearly forgot about how much danger Mom and I were in. I sat up and peeked over the top of the boulder we were hiding behind.

The supercomputer, it turned out, wasn't mistaken. Fred—*my* Fred—was there, a handful of feet beyond and a bit to the side of the front of the boulder. I instantly recognized the pattern on top of the little guy's shell. He was inching his way across the dry, dusty ground, toward a leaf about twenty-five times his size. Fred must've thought he'd hit the jackpot—the leaf looked like the world's biggest piece of lettuce.

Fred was so excited, he didn't even seem to notice the *ridiculously enormous dinosaur* hulking there a short ways away. The turtle didn't even turn from the lettuce when the creature took another earth-shaking step toward him. Because, yeah—the dinosaur seemed to have temporarily forgotten about Mom and me. Now it was headed for *Fred*.

"NO!"

It wasn't me shouting.

It was Mom.

And she wasn't shouting at the dinosaur.

She was shouting at *me*.

Because as soon as I'd realized that the dinosaur was on his way to devour Fred, I darted out from behind the boulder and got between it and my pet.

You might be wondering: What in the

world I was thinking? But the truth is, I wasn't thinking at all. My body just kicked into gear and carried me along. It was only *then*, once I'd gotten to where my body wanted me to go, that my brain caught up. And at that point it didn't really matter if I could think or not. Because it was way too late to actually *do* anything. I was now close enough to the dinosaur that it could simply bend over and snatch me up in its gigantic, drooly jaws.

And the thing looked ready to do exactly that.

The creature leaned down as far as it could, then brought its enormous, SUV-sized head right up in front of mine. Terrifyingly, I could feel the warm, meaty air blowing into and out of its nasty-looking nostrils.

The creature's gross nose-breeze slowed the drops of sweat that had begun to drip down on my forehead.

I didn't know what else to do, so I simply stood there and waited to meet my fate.

Chapter Sixteen

HAVE YOU EVER HEARD SOMEONE SAY THAT their life flashed before their eyes? People say that can happen in the midst of a super-scary situation.

Well, I was definitely in the midst of a super-scary situation. And something *did* flash before my eyes. Not my whole life, though—only a little bit of it. Specifically, the bit from a few minutes ago, after I'd first found out that Mom had accidentally sent us sixty-or-so million years too far back in time. When I'd, you know, said that thing about wishing she could be a *normal* mom. . . .

I kept hearing what I'd said over and over again, and feeling worse about it with every repetition. And getting eaten by a dinosaur was bad enough. But getting eaten by a dinosaur while my mom thought I didn't appreciate her—that was about sixty-or-so million times worse. If it was the last thing I did, I was going to make sure she knew I appreciated her a whole lot—*because of* the way she was, not in spite of it.

"Mom," I said. "About before." I paused

for a second as the dinosaur leaned even closer, its nostrils opening and closing and sucking up my scent, the wind it was making causing my stinky T-shirt to flap around a bit. "What I said," I told her, searching for right words as the dinosaur, I could only assume, searched for best part of me to sink its teeth into. "It wasn't—I didn't—I just—I was so—"

    I stopped my blathering because, out of nowhere, the dinosaur had jerked backward. It then rose up to its full height and swung its head from side to side, almost like it was trying to swat away a bee. After which it threw its head back and sent an earsplitting shriek up at the sky.

It was the worst sound I'd ever heard. Like ten billion nails scraping across a mile-long chalkboard. It made my head throb and my stomach cinch up.

Luckily, it didn't last long.

The dinosaur lowered its head, then swung its body around and—incredibly—began to run away.

I watched the creature go, feeling a weird mix of emotions. I was happy, obviously, and wildly relieved. But I was also seriously confused.

Mom was too. And so was TED.

"How . . . ," Mom said, not even sure how to ask the question.

Meanwhile, TED said, "That was highly improbable."

"You can say that again," I told him. Then I grabbed the bottom of my T-shirt and hiked it up to wipe my sweaty forehead. In the process, I got a whiff of the thing—and discovered that traveling tens of millions of years back in time and fleeing a dinosaur had made the shirt smell even worse than it already had. Bad enough to have probably made the *dinosaur's* life flash before *its* eyes. Poor thing.

In any case, it made *me* gag.

And I guess that cleared up any confusion Mom and TED had had about the dinosaur's sudden retreat.

"Ha!" Mom said. "I suppose you could say we were *saved by the smell*, huh?"

I didn't need to look to know that she was grinning.

A moment later, TED used his ultra-powerful brain to turn Mom's words into a little song. "Saaaaaved by the *smell*!" he chanted in his annoying accent. And then Mom—now fully laughing—broke out into some sort of herky-jerky victory dance. "Saaaaaved by the *smell*! Saaaaaved by the smeh-eh-eh-eh-*ell*!"

I ignored them. I scooped Fred up, then tore off a hunk of that leaf he'd been after. He chomped away at it in the safety of my hands while Mom danced and TED sang.

"*Hey*," I finally said, loud enough to stop

Mom and TED's celebration. "Shouldn't we, like, *get out of here* before any more dinosaurs come along?"

Mom winked at me and said, "So long as you keep your shirt on, I think we'll be fine." But then she pulled the pieces of the broken remote control out of her pocket and arranged them on the ground. "All right," she said. "Let's see if we can get ourselves back home."

Chapter Seventeen

IT TOOK MOM AND TED ABOUT TWENTY minutes to figure out how to get the remote working again. It wasn't *fixed*, exactly. But they were pretty sure the thing was in good enough shape to get us back home.

TED said, "If the remote malfunctions in the middle of the process, the loop may not be able to get us all the way back to our present time."

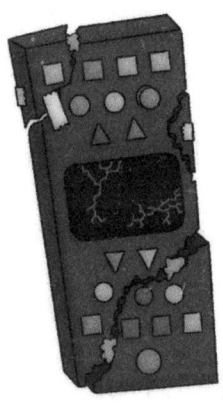

This was concerning, obviously. But wherever we ended up, I was pretty sure it couldn't be any worse than the Cretaceous period. Even if we only made it back to the 1900s, at least there were cars and movies and stuff back then.

Mom studied the repaired remote, "I

think it'll hold," she told TED. Then, to me, she said, "Remember. We have to be quick. The loop won't stay open long. Maybe only a couple of seconds."

"Got it," I said. "Be quick."

I tightened my grip on Fred, then bent my knees. I was ready to spring into action. To dart forward and dive into the patch of swirling air as soon as it showed up.

Mom counted down from three.

And then, lightning fast, she pressed a series of buttons on the remote.

POP!

A thin purplish haze appeared before us. Then . . .

WHOOSH!

All at once the purply air started swirling, as fast as a washing machine in the middle of its spin cycle.

"GO! GO! GO!" Mom cried.

I ran.

Then dove.

And after another quick trip on that nightmarish merry-go-round, I fell—OOF!—and landed on a cold, hard surface.

I peeled my eyes open.

And here's what I saw:

An overflowing tool chest.

A cardboard box crammed full of old stuffed animals and toys.

Plus about half a dozen heaps of dirty laundry.

It was our basement.

And I was so glad to see it, I could've kissed the floor.

Instead I set Fred down on it and said, "Mom?"

"Here," she said, popping up from behind one of her worktables. She dug a hand down into the pocket of her lab coat and pulled out TED.

"Ahh," the supercomputer said. "Basement, sweet basement."

Chapter Eighteen

WE'D MADE IT BACK HOME, AND NONE OF US had ended up as part of a dinosaur's lunch.

But we still had a problem—a *laundry* problem.

My stinky shirt had saved us, sure—but that didn't change the fact that it was basically a biohazard. And Mom's lab coat? It was in seriously rough shape.

Mom was eyeing the heap of dirty clothes closest to her.

"Maybe," I said, before she could get any other ideas, "we should see if we can use Mr. Jakes's washing machine."

Mom frowned. And I knew her brain was probably already cooking up some other, more complicated—and more *dangerous*—way we could get our laundry done. But then her frown flattened out, after which it turned up into a smile.

"Sure," Mom said at last. Then she got a familiar faraway look in her eyes, adding, "That might actually free up some time for me to work on my particle disrupter later."

A *particle disrupter* didn't sound much better than a *time portal*. But I decided not to get into that.

I grabbed that box full of old stuffed animals and toys and emptied it out onto the floor. Then, gearing myself up to face the stench, I began gathering dirty clothes and dumping them into the box.

Mom found a stack of empty grocery bags and started filling those.

Together, nearly choking on the noxious fumes, we hauled our laundry up the stairs, outside, and over to Mr. Jakes's house.

Chapter Nineteen

I THINK MOST PEOPLE WOULD BE PRETTY weirded out if they opened their front door to find neighbors that they hardly even knew standing there with about seventy-five pounds of nasty T-shirts and dirty lab coats in their arms. But not Mr. Jakes. The guy looked more excited than I'd ever seen him. He grinned at us as if we'd actually shown up with one of those giant checks, made out to him for a few billion dollars.

"Come in, come in," he urged us, opening the door even more.

We hadn't even had to ask.

Mr. Jakes led us through his house. It was laid out just like ours. But besides the layout of the rooms, the place couldn't have looked more different. By which I mean that it was clean. Incredibly clean. There weren't piles of papers on the countertops or stacks of books on the floor. I didn't see any vials or beakers lying around. And the whole place smelled like baked goods and flowers.

It was clean, like I said—but also cozy. In

the living room there was a bin full of fuzzy blankets. Also pillows. There were puffy ones of all different sizes, neatly lined up along the couch.

Looking at those blankets and the pillows and that couch, the chaos of the morning caught up to me. Our trip back in time hadn't taken all that long. But it had felt way, way longer. And now I couldn't help but think about how nice it'd be to lie down and take a good long nap.

I might've even gone and done exactly that if Mr. Jakes hadn't yanked me out of my daydream by taking the box of dirty clothes from my arms.

"I'll take these," he said. "The laundry room is right through here." The guy was so kind, he whistled as he went, pretending he couldn't even smell my ridiculously stinky clothes.

He disappeared for a second, then came back to grab Mom's bags of dirty clothes.

Mom watched Mr. Jakes leave. Then she turned to me. It looked like she wanted to say something but wasn't sure how to say it.

It reminded me that I'd never finished telling her what I'd wanted to tell her before.

"I . . . I'm sorry," I told her. "About all that stuff I said before. It's just that sometimes I—"

"I know," Mom said. "I know."

She came over and wrapped me up in a hug. She squeezed me for several seconds, then stepped back, a slightly twisted look on her face.

I glanced down at my T-shirt. "Yeah. I didn't think it could smell any worse either. But here we are."

"Ari," Mom said.

I looked back up, and saw that she was holding her hand out toward me, her pinkie finger extended extra far.

"Never again will we go so long without doing laundry," she told me.

I hooked my pinkie around hers. "Deal," I said.

Mr. Jakes reappeared a moment later.

He said, "Now, who wants a cookie?"

Chapter Twenty

EVENTUALLY I SAT DOWN IN ONE OF MR. JAKES'S living room chairs.

It was even cozier than it looked.

Mom and Mr. Jakes were over on the couch. She'd accepted his offer of a cookie, and had then given me a look to let me know I should do the same. They were oatmeal raisin, the same as the ones he'd brought us earlier that morning, and even though I was fairly hungry, I still didn't really want one. But the guy was being so nice. I figured eating one of his cookies was the least I could do.

So I took a cookie, and then I took a bite. And I kind of still can't believe I'm about to say this, but the cookie—it was the best cookie I'd ever had. Hands down. No contest. After that first bite, I actually spent a minute *studying* the thing, trying to figure out what else besides raisins Mr. Jakes could've possibly put into it to make it so delicious. When I couldn't, I just went back to eating it.

Then I had a few more.

All the while, Mom and Mr. Jakes chatted on the couch. She was smiling the whole time. I'm pretty sure that at first she was doing it just to be polite. But then the smile stuck around so long, I think it had to be real.

As comfortable as I was in that big chair, with half a dozen cookies in my stomach, I eventually dozed off. I'm not sure how long I slept, but it must've been at least a couple of hours, because when I woke up, our laundry had nearly all been done. Mom and Mr. Jakes were finishing up folding the last of it.

We hauled all our clean clothes home. Right away I grabbed a fresh T-shirt and changed into it.

Mom leaned toward me and took a big sniff.

"Ah," she said. "Much better."

I picked up a clean lab coat from the pile beside me and tossed it her way.

She caught it but didn't change. Instead she stood there for a second, smiling with a familiar faraway look in her eyes. It was the look she got whenever she was having a new idea.

Uh-oh, I thought.

But it turned out that her idea had nothing to do with a new invention or experiment. Not really.

"You know what?" she said. "That was actually a very nice way to spend an afternoon. Maybe we'll go visit Mr. Jakes again sometime. If he doesn't mind."

I knew he wouldn't.

"Maybe," Mom went on, now finally turning to look at me, "we'll make this a regular thing."

To be honest, the thought of this made me feel a little weird.

But as far as Mom's ideas went, this one was super tame. I mean, there were no time portals or laser beams involved.

So I shrugged and said, "Yeah. Okay. Sure. If he'll make us more of those cookies, I'm in."

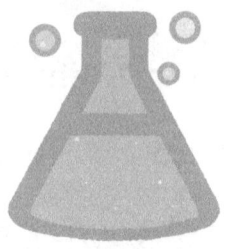

Chapter Twenty-One

THAT NIGHT, I WENT TO BED EARLY.

Which probably isn't much of a surprise.

It'd been a long and absolutely bonkers day. And that was seriously saying something, considering some of the days I'd had with Mom in the past.

Anyway, I headed to bed over an hour earlier than usual. Mom gave me an extra-long, extra-tight squeeze good night, and I didn't complain or try to wriggle my way out of it. I would've let her hug me even longer if she'd wanted to.

I carried Fred up to my room and tucked him away in his enclosure, then hit the lights and crawled into bed.

And you might be thinking that after closing my eyes and drifting off to sleep, I would have thought about dinosaurs. Or maybe one dinosaur in particular. You know, the one whose disgusting snout had been half an inch away from me. The one who'd almost *eaten me*.

But I didn't.

Instead, what I thought about was Mom. I saw her on Mr. Jakes's couch, giving our neighbor a kind of smile I hadn't seen on her face in . . .

Well, that was the thing.

I couldn't remember the last time I'd seen her smile like that.

Honestly, I couldn't remember if I'd *ever* seen her smile like that.

Which was weird.

And the fact that it'd been *Mr. Jakes* who'd gotten that smile out of her?

That was weirder still.

I thought about all this, in any case, for maybe five minutes. At which point my brain got too tired to think.

Then I fell asleep.

And then, yeah—I dreamed of dinosaurs.